Brady Brady
and the Great Exchange

Written by Mary Shaw

Illustrated by Chuck Temple

PUBLISHED BY
BRADY BRADY INC.

Visit **www.bradybrady.com** for more Brady Brady information

Published in Canada in 2004 by

Brady Brady Inc.
P.O. Box 367
Waterloo, Ontario
Canada
N2J 4A4

Canadian Cataloguing in Publication Data

ISBN 9780973555721

Before every game, Brady's friend Gregory likes to
be alone in the dressing room. His teammates understand:
they have their rituals too.

Printed and bound in Canada

Keep adding to your Brady Brady book collection! Other titles include **Brady Brady and the:**

• **Great Rink**	• **Twirling Torpedo**	• **B Team**
• **Runaway Goalie**	• **Most Important Game**	
• **Singing Tree**	• **MVP**	
• **Super Skater**	• **Puck on the Pond**	
• **Big Mistake**	• **Cranky Kicker**	

For my little rink rat, Caroline
Mary Shaw

To Dave, for your guidance and patience
Chuck Temple

It was game day and the Icehogs huddled in the center of the dressing room for their team cheer.

"We've got the power,
We've got the might,
They call us the Icehogs,
And we're outta sight!"

Then, one by one they filed
out the door giggling.
Everybody but Gregory.

At the start of the hockey season, Gregory had told his teammates that he needed a few minutes alone to focus on his game. He always remained in the dressing room while the others took to the ice to warm up. So, the Icehogs left Gregory alone. After all, they had their superstitions, too.

Brady **always** had to be the first one at the rink.

Chester would **not** play without munching on popcorn first.

Tes made her dad take the exact same route to the rink every time — avoiding all potholes and sewers.

Tree would hum as he put on his equipment — first the left side, and then the right.

When the warm-up began, Brady realized he had forgotten the water bottles and returned to the dressing room to get them. There was Gregory, cheeks puffed out, sweat rolling down his forehead, as he fought to wedge his feet into his skates.

"Are you okay, Gregory?" Brady asked his red-faced teammate.

"I . . . I'm fine, Brady Brady," answered Gregory, as he quickly wiped a sweat ball off his nose. "I'll be right out."

Brady picked up the water bottles and turned to leave. He knew his friend wasn't telling the truth. "If you don't feel well," Brady said, "maybe you shouldn't play today."

Gregory looked sadly at his friend. "I don't want to let the team down, but I can't go out there today . . . or any other day."

"What are you talking about?" Brady asked.

In barely a whisper, Gregory leaned over to Brady and said sadly, "My skates don't fit me anymore and my parents can't buy me new ones right now. It hurts to skate."

As Gregory began to pack up his equipment bag, Brady noticed his red, puffy feet. Gregory had stopped wearing his tie-dyed socks a month ago. His teammates had found this strange because Gregory had always claimed that the thick, green socks were his good luck charm. Now Brady knew what was wrong.

Brady rifled through his
equipment bag and pulled out a bottle of lotion.

"My mom put this in my bag 'cause she says my gloves give me
stinky hands. If we rub some lotion on your feet, maybe they'll
slide right into your skates!" Brady suggested. "Do you think
you could just play once more in these? Then later we can figure
out what to do."

This made Gregory **and** his feet feel much better.

Gregory tried not to think about the pain in his toes as he skated up and down the ice. But by the third period, Brady could see that his friend was hurting. He suggested that Gregory just stand in front of the net, so that Brady could pass the puck to him as much as possible.

Nobody seemed to notice anything was wrong, and both boys were relieved when the final buzzer sounded.

The Icehogs' dressing room was filled with
the usual post-game chatter.

It was Chester who gave Brady the great idea.

"I think I'd like to play with bigger arm pads," Chester said as he flexed his scrawny muscles. "I bet it would help me take up more room in the net."

"My mom would love it if I got rid of these smelly gloves," Brady chimed in. "So, I've got a *great* idea!"

Everyone stopped and listened.

"We'll have the biggest equipment exchange ever! Bring anything you can't wear anymore, and maybe you can swap it for something else!" Brady said, winking at Gregory.

The Icehogs loved the idea.

They spent the rest of the day putting up flyers around town, announcing the ***great*** hockey exchange at Brady's ***great*** backyard rink.

Brady and Gregory were so excited,
they both had trouble sleeping.

When the big day arrived, Gregory was the first one to show up, his too-small skates tucked under his arm. Brady had made signs that poked up from the snowbanks at each corner of the rink.

Gregory placed his skates under the "SKATES" sign.
People arrived from all over town.

Brady spotted the perfect pair of gloves. He was sure that they would help him score some big goals.

Chester found a big set of arm pads. He was certain nobody would be able to get anything past him.

Gregory sat patiently waiting for skates his size — the excitement on his face fading each time he checked a pair of skates that were placed under the "SKATES" sign.

All were either way too small, or way too big.

Gregory was about to give up hope when Brady walked out of his house and over to the pile, placing his own skates under the sign.

"What are you doing, Brady Brady?" Gregory asked as he picked them up. "You skate like the wind in these!"

Brady nodded. "It's time for someone else to skate like the wind in them."

Gregory's feet slid right in. "PERFECT!" they both shouted.

Gregory raced off to test out his new skates. Brady stared at the pile in front of him. None of the skates were his size. Finally, he settled for a pair and tried them on.

As Brady laced them up, Gregory skated back and pulled something out of his pocket.

"Those look a bit big, Brady Brady. Here, try these on for size," he said, proudly holding up his green, tie-dyed socks. "They'll help your skates fit and bring you good luck."

Gregory was right. The lucky socks did make Brady's feet fit better in the skates.

The streetlights were coming on as the last happy customers left
the backyard. Brady and Gregory had the whole rink to themselves.
The only equipment that nobody had wanted . . .

. . . Brady's smelly gloves.